Sylvie Marcoux

Victoria's
Monday Adventures

Illustrator
Guadalupe Trejo

Cat's Eye Collection
Phoenix Publishing

Illustrator : Guadalupe Trejo
Cover Design by: Guadalupe Trejo
Editor: Jacqueline Snider

Phoenix Publishing
206, rue Laurier
L'île-Bizard (Montréal)
(Québec) Canada H9C 2W9
Tel.:   (514) 696-7381 Fax: (514) 696-7685
www.editionsduphoenix.com

Bibliothèque et Archives nationales du Québec and Library
and Archives Canada cataloguing in publication

Marcoux, Sylvie, 1967-

        [Lundis de Victoria. English]

        Victoria's Monday Adventures

        (Eye-of-the-cat)
        Translation of: Les lundis de Victoria.
        For children aged 9 to 12.

        ISBN 978-2-9234-2594-8

        I. Trejo, Guadalupe. II. Laubitz, Zofia, 1958-   . III.
Title. IV. Title: Lundis de Victoria. English.

PS8576.A642L8613 2009   jC843'.6 C2009-941859-2
PS9576.A642L8613 2009

Phoenix Publishing acknowledges the support for its
publishing program provided by the
Government of Canada through the Book Publishing
Industry Development Program and the
Canada Council for the Arts, and the province of Quebec
for its financial support through SODEC.

Sylvie Marcoux

Victoria's Monday Adventures

Translated by

Zofia Laubitz

Phoenix Publishing

Acknowledgements

I would like to thank everyone who, directly and indirectly, helped me write Victoria's Monday Adventures. I won't mention their names in alphabetical order, but instead in chronological order.

First of all, I would like to thank my Grade Four elementary school teacher, Madame Françoise, who was my inspiration and whose name I have used. Then, in Grade Five, there was a Mademoiselle Rollande, who knew everything, who had eyes in the back of her head, who scared me to death, but who had a big heart. A character in this book also inherited the gentleness, warmth and love of life of Sister Céline, my Grade Six teacher, who absolutely adored the French language. Sister Céline and Sister Marie (my Third Grade teacher) introduced me to the pleasures of discovering and playing with words. Later, in Grade Eleven, there was Jacques Girard, French teacher and author. With his help, I learned to use words to tell stories. Jacques, don't look for yourself in this story; I'm keeping you for another book, although... you share your gift of gab with a character in this novel!

I would like to thank André, my husband, my friend and my love, for being there.

I would like to thank my daughters, Audrey-Anne and Marilou, my sister Hélène, and my mother Yvonne, my first and most faithful readers.

Many thanks to my colleague Céline for her eight pages of valuable and thoughtful comments. Without you, Céline, Victoria's Monday Adventures would still be in draft form.

I would like to thank Jean for introducing me to the *Tablée populaire*.

Thank you my dear Aunt Micheline for your eagle eyes and the pride I see in them, which gives me the courage to continue and to always look on the bright side.

Thank you, Virginie, for your enthusiasm. You have the power to make people believe that anything is possible.

And finally, I would like to thank, from the bottom of my heart, Liliane and her wonderful team at Éditions du Phoenix. Right from the beginning, I felt encouraged in this adventure and accepted into her beautiful literary family.

Sylvie

To my two beautiful big girls,
Audrey-Anne and Marilou

TABLE OF CONTENTS

CHAPTER 1

School

"Victoria! Charles! Edward! Hurry up or you'll be late for The Club."

"Yes, Mom! I just have to fix my hair and grab my school bag and I'll be ready."

Every day, since the start of the school year, Victoria and the twins attended the Quebec Breakfast Club, known as The Club. The Club's mission is to give all schoolchildren a chance to eat breakfast before classes start in the morning.

The first time their mother talked to them about it, they refused to sign up. They were afraid of being laughed at. Afraid that the other kids would tease them, saying they were poor. They were poor, yes, but they were proud too. Finally, after some discussion, they agreed to try it, just for a week. To their surprise, on their first morning, they saw that children from all social classes, without exception, attended The Club.

They made new friends very quickly. For example, they met Emily, who never felt hungry when she woke up so breakfast at school was the ideal solution for her. Matthew's mother was seriously ill and Oliver was the son of Madame Carstairs, the school principal.

"Okay, I'm ready," called Victoria. "Boys, I'm waiting. It's time to go if we want to get there on time."

Turning to her mother, Victoria asked, "Did you have a good night at work?"

Each Thursday through Sunday, Isabelle worked in a big restaurant. After the restaurant closed for the night, she cleaned and prepared the rooms so everything was ready when it opened early the next morning.

"Yes, everything went well. And you?"

"Charles and Edward slept like angels. Elizabeth had a nightmare and wet her bed that's why she's sleeping in ours. I put her sheets to soak. I'll come back at lunchtime and hang them out on the line."

"No, no. It's lunchtime, stay at school, I'll take care of the laundry. You already help me so much. If you want to make me happy, concentrate on your studies. That's important!"

"Yes, Mom."

"Have a good day! I love you."

"I love you too, Mom. Are you coming, boys?"

With her nose pressed against the kitchen window of their tiny apartment, Isabelle watched her three eldest children disappear in the direction of the school. She was so lucky to have kids like them.

Victoria, a tall pretty brunette, was very sensible for her age. She turned twelve on May 24th. Because she was

born on Queen Victoria's birthday, her parents decided to give her the Queen's name.

Victoria was older than the other kids in her class. After her father died in a car accident she had to repeat a year of school. The terrible tragedy occurred almost three years ago, exactly one month before Elizabeth was born. When she was in Grade Five for the first time, Victoria was still a child. When she was in Grade Five for the second time, she seemed to have aged five years.

Isabelle sighed deeply thinking how much she would have loved to give her children a better life. Unfortunately, fate had decided differently. Still, she kept her hopes up. In the last year, their quality of life had greatly improved thanks to the assistance offered by the school.

In addition to the Quebec Breakfast Club, where her three eldest were able to eat for very little money five days a week, they also benefited from a lunch program. When they arrived at school, the children put their lunch bags away in a common refrigerator. While they were in class, volunteers replaced the lunch bags with others that looked identical. The only difference was that the new lunch bags contained healthy, balanced meals. Isabelle knew that Victoria had figured out the trick long ago, but the boys hadn't.

When the twins started Grade One, Isabelle had more time to rest. She took advantage of the fact that Elizabeth wasn't an early riser to relax a bit when she got home from work. She also took a nap in the afternoon with the toddler and slept for an hour or two before going to work. That was lucky, since working at night wasn't ideal for a mother raising four kids by herself. But the job allowed them to survive, while she looked for something better.

Isabelle picked up the transmitter-receiver and called Madame Beausoleil, their neighbour. She thanked her and turned off the intercom between the two apartments. It made Isabelle feel better to know that the kind woman could hear everything that was going on while she was out.

Tired, she trudged to the bedroom where Elizabeth was sleeping peacefully. When asleep, the beautiful blond toddler looked like an angel. It was a good idea to take advantage of the time before she woke up and turned back into a little devil!

Isabelle finally slid into bed and fell asleep, cuddling her daughter's warm little body against her own.

CHAPTER 2

Victoria's Walks

Once a week, on Monday, Victoria was allowed to go out after supper. She usually took the opportunity to go to the public library. As often as possible, she would take a different route, which gave her the chance to explore her quiet little town a bit.

While she was strolling along the sidewalk, she would peek cautiously into the lighted windows. She would find inspiration in what she saw, imagining people's lives and events, in other words, making up stories. Victoria sometimes wondered if her family would be happier if they lived in one of the luxurious houses instead of their apartment. Even though she really loved her mom, her brothers and her sister, Victoria felt smothered in the tiny rooms of their apartment.

She dreamed of having a bedroom of her own one day. It didn't matter whether it was big or small. A little bedroom would suit her fine, with a bed covered with a pink-flowered bedspread, where she would sleep all alone and where, through the lace-curtained window, she could watch the clouds drift across the sky. She didn't want a computer or a television. She would be happy with a table, a chair, some pencils and huge sheets of white paper so she could draw and draw and draw some more. For Victoria, that would be more than enough to make her happy.

Victoria had a natural talent for drawing. When she was drawing, nothing else existed around her. It was as if she were transported to another world. To a marvellous place where she lived with the characters she created with her pencil. Her characters, both men and women, had the faces and clothing of the people she saw through the windows of their homes or sometimes met on the street during her Monday evening walks.

Unfortunately, if she was drawing at home, and Elizabeth was nearby, her return to reality was often jarring! That's why Victoria would have liked to have a place all to herself.

This Monday, her feet took her to a part of town that she was particularly fond of, an area that was partly commercial and partly residential. After crossing several intersections, she found herself close to a printing shop. Victoria approached the building as if she were attracted by a magnet. It was a warm Indian-summer evening and the doors of the pressroom were wide open. A man dressed in overalls was working on a huge rotary press while whistling happily. Mountains of paper were piled here and there. At one end of the press the paper was white, and at the other end it was covered in bright colours. Suddenly, the pressman leaned over and, with a quick motion, pulled a copy out of the machine's jaws. He straightened up and examined it carefully. From where she was standing, Victoria caught a glimpse of a magnificent landscape.

"Hey, you! What are you doing here? Are you looking for someone? Can I help you?"

Victoria jumped. A woman wearing faded jeans and a loose, colourful blouse gracefully walked towards her.

"No, no. I was attracted by the noise and then the colours, the paper... it's magical!"

"That's true. When I started working here, I found everything amazing too. Magical, as you said."

"Have you been working here long?"

"Oh... for... hmm... let me think. Um, I've been a graphic designer for this company for almost fifteen years. The profession has changed a lot since I started. In those days, we used pens called rapidographs. Now, we only use computers. The work of graphic design used to be more artistic than it is now."

"You sound quite nostalgic!"

"You're right. This evening we happen to be reorganizing the design department. It breaks my heart to throw out all the old materials, but we don't have a choice. Soon we will be receiving our new equipment and we have to make room for it."

"You're throwing out your pens, India ink and all that stuff?"

"Yes, none of that is any use to us anymore. As I was saying, the computer..."

"Could I have them?" interrupted Victoria, her eyes bright with hope.

"The old materials? Sure, but what will you do with them?"

"I'll draw pictures," replied Victoria without hesitation. She could hardly believe her luck.

"Okay, wait here for a few minutes. I'll be back. Don't go near the press because it can be dangerous."

"No, I won't."

A few minutes later, the graphic designer came back with a box full of drawing pads, pencils, rulers, compasses, bottles of ink and pens. Tears of joy filled Victoria's big blue eyes.

"Oh! Thank you! Thank you!"

"I'm happy to do it. I'm pleased to know that you'll give new life to these good old work tools. In fact, what's your name?"

"Victoria. And yours?"

"Julie. So, my dear Victoria, don't forget to come back and show me your work."

"I promise, I won't forget! And thanks again!"

Back on the sidewalk, Victoria felt as if she were floating on air rather than walking. She was so happy. It was one of the best days of her life.

But where could she keep her gift? Not at home, it was too small, and if Elizabeth ever got her hands on it that would be the end of her treasure.

It was getting late and if she wanted to get some books at the library Victoria needed to find a hiding place for her treasure quickly. What if she put them in the old, abandoned house on Laurier Street, just for the night? She had taken shelter there a few weeks ago when she was caught in the rain. The two-story building was actually an old carpentry workshop, which hadn't been in use for quite some time. Old tools were stored on the ground floor, but the attic was almost empty. The double doors in front were locked with a huge rusty padlock, but the lock on the back door was broken. That's how Victoria had gotten in.

On the evening of the storm, she had read on the mailbox that the building belonged to someone named Françoise Ouellet. Victoria had heard that name before. She was a woman who had taught her mother when she was in elementary school. The former teacher had a reputation for being a real 'dragon woman'!

But that wasn't important now because all Victoria needed was a safe place to hide her new drawing materials. And anyway, she'd come back the next day and get them.

CHAPTER 3

The Discovery

"Say, Mom, can I go over to Emily's tonight? We want to work on our oral presentation."

"Sure."

As soon as supper was over and the dishes were washed, Victoria dashed out of the apartment. She was a bit ill at ease. It was the first time she had ever hidden anything from her mother. She really did have to go over to her friend's house to practice their language arts presentation, but before that she wanted to go and retrieve her box. The problem was that she didn't have anywhere else to put it. But she'd find a place.

As she passed the printing shop she slowed down. The evening air was cool and the pressroom doors were closed. It was too bad. Victoria stopped for a moment and leaned against the wall. She could hear the purring of the presses and feel the vibrations of the machines. What were they printing today? Books? Concert posters? Or reproductions of art like yesterday? She really wanted to know. She also wanted to watch the huge presses again as they made a picture appear, one colour after another. What if she sneaked in silently? The doors might not be locked. But no. The day before, Julie had warned her that it was dangerous.

Victoria noticed the big blue recycling bins just to her left. They were lined up one after the other and linked together with a chain. She hadn't noticed them before, she'd been concentrating on what might be going on inside the print shop. One of the bins was overflowing with colourful pages. One of the pages looked familiar. Victoria walked over and pulled on it gently. It was a copy of the reproduction that had impressed her so much the day before. Since the printed page was going to be recycled anyway, she decided to keep it. She rolled it up carefully, proud of her new find, and walked back to the old carpenter's workshop where she had hidden the box with her precious art materials.

When she arrived, Victoria made sure no one could see her and then climbed up to the attic. Right away, she felt comfortable there. It was so peaceful. The moon, full and round like a cheese, lit up the dormer window. The sound of the wind caressed the boards on the walls, which had grown grey with age. She felt as if she had finally found a place of her own.

It wasn't too damp and there was even electricity! She decided to turn on the light bulb hanging from the ceiling, since there were no side windows facing old Madame Ouellet's house. Even better, there were no neighbours at all behind the building, just a field and a small thicket of alders.

Victoria decided to explore the attic from one end to the other. In one corner she found a wooden bench that was quite

solid. She carried it over to the window, blew on it to remove the dust and then sat down. Her eyes scanned the room once again. When she saw the layer of dust covering the floor and dozens of spiderwebs hanging here and there, she figured that nobody ever went there. Suddenly, she had an idea. Why not tidy it up? She wouldn't do any damage or break anything. She would just make the place look nicer. With a little effort and a good cleaning, she could turn this abandoned attic into an artist's studio.

Victoria stood up and went to get the big piece of recycled paper she'd left near the door. Her heart was pounding. The day before, she hadn't been able to see the reproduction in detail. "How beautiful it is!" she thought. Under a clear blue sky, a meadow stretched away into the distance. Among the soft green blades of grass, delicate wildflowers were growing here and there. But what held Victoria's attention the most was the willow tree on the right side of the picture. It was huge, and its gnarled branches were twisted and bent down towards the ground. It looked ancient, sad and alone.

With some rusty nails, Victoria pinned the picture to the grey plank wall. She sat down again on the wooden bench, rested her chin on her hands and lost herself in the picture. She sighed deeply; she hadn't felt that good in a long, long time. Unfortunately, a barking dog brought her back to reality. She had to go! Emily was waiting for her so they could practice their presentation.

CHAPTER 4

Moving In

For several weeks, every Monday evening, instead of going to the library Victoria went to the attic. The attic had become her refuge. With a lot of effort and imagination, she gradually transformed it into a studio.

More than once, luck came her way. In fact, almost every time she went to the attic, Victoria discovered something useful in the former schoolteacher's garbage. One evening, Madame Ouellet threw out a drawing table. Victoria quickly sneaked it away and carried it up, with some difficulty, to the second floor.

Thanks to Madame Ouellet's eccentricities, which were helping Victoria without her knowing it, the attic soon became a friendly place. A pretty curtain, not pink like Victoria's daydreams, but sky-blue, decorated the window. Pictures adorned the walls. A lamp lit up her drawing table. It was beautiful, warm and, above all, clean.

October gave way to November. Victoria always waited for her Mondays with impatience. Now that her cleaning and decorating were complete, as soon as she arrived at her secret hideout, she would rush to open the box containing the artist's materials the designer had given her and start drawing. She made the most of those moments when she could let herself go, forget everything and do what she loved. The drawing table was almost completely covered with sketches. Soon, she would go and show them to Julie. But not yet. Victoria didn't feel ready. Next week? Maybe. But, in the meantime, she could... yes, she could...

CHAPTER 5

The Meeting

It was already the beginning of the second week of November and it was very cold. The evening air smelled like snow. Bundled up well in her warm clothes with her nose buried in her woollen scarf, Victoria walked into the wind. Actually, she wasn't even aware of the elements, she was already thinking of her attic and her drawings. The previous week, after hesitating a long time, she had finally decided to reproduce the landscape she'd found in the recycling bin. With her lead pencil, Victoria drew the horizon line. She sketched the willow, the bouquets of daisies and the sprays of buttercups. Then, she

had paused, concerned. Victoria wanted to add a person so that the tree would be less alone. But who should she draw? Her mother? The twins? Elizabeth? Her father? Her father... but what if she couldn't remember what he looked like? With tears pouring down her cheeks and a heavy heart, she'd put away her pencils and her sketch. She decided to continue the picture the next Monday.

Victoria finally felt ready to draw the people. Helped in by a gust of wind, she entered the back door of the building and ran up the steps leading to the attic two at a time. She paused for a moment to catch her breath. Then she took off her mittens, her scarf, her hat and her coat, which she threw on the rocking chair near the door. She took three steps to the pull-chain for the light and pulled on it. The light bulb lit up the room... Victoria let out a blood-curdling scream!

On the chair, buried under Victoria's woollen clothes, sat a tiny white-haired woman.

"My goodness! Madame Ouellet?" It was crazy all the things a person could think of in just a few seconds. "That's it, I've been caught. The former teacher will call the police. I'll spend the night in jail. Mom will never let me go out again... even if the police let me out of jail. No more drawing. My life is over!"

Victoria felt like a hunted animal. She didn't dare move a muscle, afraid that the least movement would shatter her corner of paradise.

"Good evening. What's your name?" asked the woman in a soft voice.

"Phew!"

The tension eased ever so slightly.

"V...Vic...Victoria."

"Oh! What a pretty name! I'm Françoise Ouellet. You can call me Madame Françoise."

"I know who you are. You're the owner of this building."

"You're very well-informed, young lady."

"I read your name on the mailbox. I also know that you used to teach my mother."

"Really? What's her name?"

"Isabelle Mercier."

"Isabelle Mercier... yes, I remember her. Very well, in fact. Now that I think of it, you look a lot like her. You've got the same blue eyes. Your mother was a rebellious child. Always insisting that this or that had to change. She was quite a handful, but I have to admit that, in most cases, she was right."

"My mother? Rebellious? You must be thinking of someone else. Mom never complains at all, even when life is unfair."

"Well, maybe that's exactly it, life has something to do with it. But getting back to us."

"Uh, right... us," answered Victoria, suddenly feeling uncomfortable.

"I don't know where to start," said the old woman, scratching her chin. "Right! First of all, don't just stand there in the middle of the room like a bump on a log, you'll take root. Here, take your clothes and put them on the table. I'm hot under your coat. Then pull the bench over and sit down next to me," ordered Madame Françoise in her schoolteacher's voice.

Victoria did what the woman asked. In any case, she didn't have much choice. She'd been caught in the act. Legally, she had no right to be in the attic and even less right to set up her studio in it. She sat down on the bench and crossed her hands in her lap to stop them from trembling.

"Now, young lady," continued the owner, in a stern voice that made Victoria shudder, "were you ever planning on telling me that you had taken up residence in the attic of my father's old carpentry shop?"

"No."

"No? Ah! Well, at least that's an honest answer. I like that. I also love what you've done with this room. We've decorated it well, haven't we?"

"We?"

"Of course, we. Did you think it was just by chance that I put all these things in the garbage over the last few weeks? That

I had the heating system repaired? Didn't you find it was a bit strange to discover all these things?"

"Well, yes... a bit... I just thought that you were wasteful... excuse me, I didn't mean to say that!"

"But you did say it."

"You mean you knew everything from the start? How did you find out?"

"Young woman, you'll find that I know everything! When I was a teacher, I was known for having eyes in the back of my head. When I was writing on the blackboard, I could always tell who was listening, who was clowning around and who was daydreaming. Your mother, by the way, spent her time drawing cartoons. She would wait until my back was turned to pass them around the class."

"My mother? Drawing? I didn't know she could draw."

"Yes, and she had a lot of talent. But getting back to us."

"Okay," said Victoria, her mind wandering.

"Getting back to us, getting back to us! It's so frustrating after all. For once

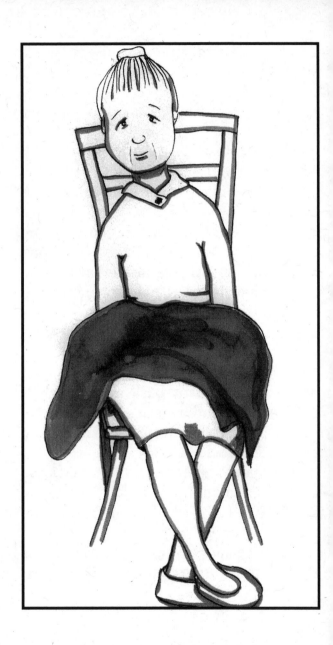

someone is telling me about my mother!" she thought.

"Since you were honest with me, I'll be honest with you."

Victoria was eager to find out how the old woman had discovered that she'd tidied up the attic. And she wouldn't have long to wait because the woman was a real chatterbox!

"It was at the beginning of October, the fourth, no, the second... or was it the fifth? I'm not sure. Ah yes, I remember, it was the third. But the exact date isn't important, is it?"

Madame Françoise resumed her soliloquy without giving Victoria the chance to utter a single word. Victoria was feeling a bit overwhelmed as the flood of words crashed over her. It really wasn't easy to follow this odd little woman's conversation.

"Anyway, I was in the kitchen making a cup of tea. I always have some tea in the evening. It aids my digestion. Some people say that... oh, I won't bore you with all that. We don't have all night! Simply, I was in the kitchen, when I suddenly saw a beam of light reflected in the field. At first glance, I thought it was a moonbeam, but the path of light wasn't shining in the right direction. Then I realized it was coming from the attic. That worried me. I thought a gang of criminals was up to no good. I watched the backyard for a long time, hidden behind my curtains. And imagine my surprise when I saw a young woman emerge instead of a group of trouble-makers."

"Why didn't you call the police?"

"Why? Oh, because I was having too much fun," answered Madame Françoise, giggling.

Victoria was astonished to see this strange woman laughing like a little girl. Her mother's old teacher wasn't at all like her mother had said she was!

"You know," continued the old woman in a confidential voice, "while I was hiding behind the curtain, I imagined so many possibilities! The time passed so quickly, I even forgot to drink my tea! The next day, as soon as the sun came up, I came to the attic. I was curious to find out what you'd been doing up here. I rummaged around a bit and discovered your drawing materials, and on my second visit, I found this wonderful picture. But tell me Victoria, why did you hide these things here? Did you steal them?" she added, sounding stern again.

"Absolutely not! Julie, the graphic designer at the Paper Plus print shop, gave them to me. You can call her. She will confirm it. She was going to throw them out."

"I believe you. But why did you leave them here?"

"Because at home we have no space for them."

"Do you have a big family?"

"Yes," answered Victoria. "There's my little sister Elizabeth. She's terrible! Then the twins, Charles and Edward."

"It doesn't surprise me at all that you have all been named after British monarchs! As a child, your mother was fascinated by royalty. As far as I can see, she hasn't changed."

"That's true! I never noticed that before!"

"You seem to love your family a lot," added Madame Françoise gently.

"Oh yes! Did you know that my brothers are very special?"

"No, what's so extraordinary about them?"

"They're real twins, but they weren't born on the same day, or in the same month, or in the same year, or even in the same century!"

"Now, my dear Victoria, you're telling me a big lie and I don't like that. I appreciated your honesty."

"Madame Françoise, I swear it's true! Charles was born at 11:55 p.m. on December 31, 2000, while Edward was born at 12:05 a.m. on January 1, 2001."

"So, you're right, they really are special!" said Madame Françoise, laughing. She was pleased to find out that the girl hadn't lied to her. "Well, I have to leave you now or you won't have any time to draw. See you soon!"

The old woman got out of the rocking chair painfully, and walked slowly to the attic door.

"Madame Françoise?"
"Yes, Victoria?"
"Thank you for letting me use your attic."
"It's my pleasure," she answered as her face lit up with a gentle smile.

Once alone, Victoria hurried to retrieve the landscape sketch she had started the Monday before. She didn't have much time before she too had to leave, but she felt inspired that evening after her strange meeting. Her pencil danced across the paper. Different but not yet well-defined figures took shape. The old willow wasn't alone anymore.

CHAPTER 6

The Confession

"Mom! I'm back!" the girl called out happily.

"Victoria? Would you come here, please?"

"Yes, Mom! I just have to hang up my coat and I'll be there."

"Sit down on the bed. I want to talk to you about something important."

From the tone of her mother's voice, Victoria sensed something was wrong. "Is she going to tell me she has to work on Christmas Eve? Or that she's lost her job? Or worse... that Charles is sick again?"

"Victoria... I think you're hiding something from me."

"Oh no, Mom."

"Don't lie to me. This evening, I phoned Emily's house to ask you to stop at the grocery store to pick up some milk and she said you weren't there."

"It's just that..."

"Let me finish please. Then I called the library and they told me you weren't there either. The librarian even told me that you hadn't been at the library, as I had thought, for several weeks. Is that true?"

"Well..."

"So where are you going?"

"Oh, Mom, don't get mad. I was going to tell you about it tonight."

"Is that so?"

"Yes, Mom, you have to believe me."

For a whole hour, Victoria told her mother about meeting Julie the designer, the discovery of the reproduction in the recycling bin and the effect the drawing had on her. Then she told her how she had decorated the attic with the objects she'd found in the garbage and, finally, her meeting earlier that evening with the strange Madame Françoise.

"You're not telling me that the attic belongs to Françoise Ouellet, Fussy Françoise?"

"Yes. She's really nice, you know."

"Oh, you must have made a mistake. We can't be talking about the same person!"

Victoria started to laugh.

"I said exactly the same thing when she talked about you. Mom? Is it true that you can draw?"

"I used to draw. I don't now."

"Why did you stop?"

"No time, no room, no interest."

"I see. Did you keep any of your drawings?"

"Yes, they're put away in a box somewhere. I'll show them to you someday, but not tonight. It's already late," said Isabelle, in a voice that meant the discussion was over.

Victoria didn't press the matter. She was used to this kind of reaction from her mother. Whenever she asked her about her youth, Isabelle refused to answer. This evening wasn't the right time, maybe it would never be the right time.

Her mother stood up, kissed Victoria on the forehead and walked heavily towards the bedroom door.

"Mom?"

"Yes?" said Isabelle, turning to reveal a face full of regret.

"Thank you for listening to me. I love you."

"I love you too, sweetie. Go to bed now, if you want to be well-rested for school tomorrow."

CHAPTER 7

The Tea Party

♬ *"Dashing through the snow, on a one-horse open sleigh..."* ♬

On her way to the attic, Victoria was surprised to find herself cheerfully humming a Christmas carol. It was the first time she'd done that in two years.

Christmas was the time of year she hated the most. No, not the most. The worst was January, when it was time to go back to school after the long holiday. The first hour of school began with the teacher asking every student to talk about his or her best memory from the holidays, Victoria didn't enjoy that at all.

The previous year she'd been able to avoid it because she had the flu, a gift from Charles. Victoria pushed away her negative thoughts. After all, the holidays had only started a few days ago. She would have lots of time to think things over in January.

That morning, as Edward had said when he woke up, there were only two more nights until Christmas Eve. Victoria's heart moved between sadness and joy.

She was sad because she wouldn't be able to go back to her attic for a few weeks. It wasn't that she was being punished for hiding the attic's existence from her mom. Not at all. It was because over the next few days Isabelle would be working at the restaurant more often and, while she was working, Victoria would have to look after her brothers and sister. As well, they would have to prepare for the Christmas celebrations and the twins' birthday party. Isabelle and Victoria were determined to make the special occasions unforgettable for the children, despite their lack of money.

Victoria was happier because things were going better now that her mother knew about the attic. The weight of the secret had become a heavy burden. She was relieved to no longer have anything to hide. She was happy for another reason too. Whenever she visited her attic, Madame Françoise, sitting comfortably in the rocking chair, welcomed her. Victoria waited with impatience for the time they spent together. She loved listening to the old woman's stories. Victoria didn't have to ask twice for Madame Françoise to tell her stories about her life!

Victoria raced up the stairs, which creaked and moaned in a sinister way. But that didn't slow her down. She was eager to see Madame Françoise again because she had a surprise for her. A Christmas gift. A little present thanking her for allowing her to use the attic, but also for the time that Madame Françoise spent

with her, which had become precious to Victoria. She knew how lucky she was.

She flung open the door, but her high spirits were dashed by the silence that filled the room. Madame Françoise wasn't waiting for her in the rocking chair! Victoria had been so impatient to get there that she hadn't noticed that the attic was completely dark. She pulled on the chain and the light bulb's glow revealed a pink envelope on the table with her name elegantly written on it. Despite her excitement, she picked it up gently and opened it very carefully so she didn't rip it. On a pink card that matched the envelope, she read,

Dear Victoria,
I'm waiting for you at my house for tea.
Madame F.

Victoria raced down the stairs. Halfway down, she realized she'd forgotten the present she wanted to give

Madame Françoise. She raced back up, got the beautifully wrapped box out of its hiding place and turned off the light for the fourth time. "Hurry! Hurry!"

At the threshold of the adjoining house, Victoria nervously grabbed hold of the impressive door knocker. It was made of gilded metal shaped like a lion's head. She knocked on the door to the rhythm of her pounding heart.

"Is that you, Victoria?" called Madame Françoise.
"Yes. Hello!"
"Hang up your coat on the rack and come and join me in the living room, it's the first door on your right."

Victoria found the large entrance hall intimidating. It was almost as big as the room that Elizabeth and the twins slept in. Right in front of her was an imposing staircase made of dark wood. She put her gift down on an antique table, next to a crystal vase full of roses. Then she stuffed her hat and mittens into the sleeve of her coat and hung it up on the rack, as Madame Françoise had asked. When she turned around, she could see her reflection in a magnificent oval mirror with a gilded frame. Her cheeks were rosy red and her eyes were shining. She found it hard to believe that it was really her, Victoria Mercier-Laporte, who she could see in the mirror in the middle of such elegant surroundings. Unsure, she stayed on the splendid hall carpet, not daring to move.

"Are you coming?"
"Yes... oh... yes, I'm coming," she replied, waking as if from a dream.

Victoria nervously tidied her long brown hair while walking in the direction of Madame Françoise's voice.

The sitting room was even more impressive than the hallway. The walls were covered in old rose and cream-coloured wallpaper. At the end of the room there was a superb black grand piano. To the right there was a stone fireplace, where a large fire was burning, warming up the room. Seated on one of two velvet sofas, Madame Françoise waited patiently, giving Victoria the time to take in her surroundings.

"Very well. Have you seen everything? Do you like it? Choose a teacup for yourself from the cabinet with the glass door and come and sit near me," she ordered, in her schoolteacher's voice.

"Pardon me? But why are all the cups different?"

"Ah, you know, I'm old and sentimental. Each one I bought during a trip abroad or for a special occasion. Since every city and every occasion is unique, every teacup has to be too. Don't you think?"

"Yes, but there are dozens."

"Go ahead! Choose one."

Victoria hesitated. She thought they were all beautiful. Finally, she chose a delicate white porcelain cup decorated with pink and lavender flowers.

"Ah! You've surprised me. I was sure you'd choose the one with the border of little red, yellow and orange diamonds, which I discovered in a market in Mexico. It matches your cheerful, spontaneous personality."

"Well, that one's beautiful too. I hesitated between the two."

"Do you like tea?"

"I don't know. I've never tried it."

"Put your cup on the table."

Victoria sat down on the other sofa and watched as Madame Françoise held the teapot very high above the cups and filled them with a graceful, practiced gesture. Victoria was very impressed.

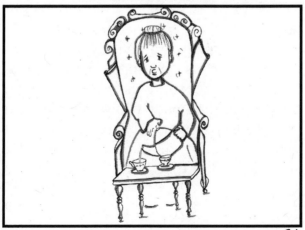

"You can add milk and sugar if you like. I take mine black."

"Then I will too."

To hide her uncertainty, Victoria leaned towards the low table, picked up her cup and imitated the old woman by dipping her lips into the hot liquid. She almost made a face. The tea was very bitter. She should have added some sugar.

"Madame Françoise?"

"Yes?"

"Can you tell me the story of the cup I chose?"

"Oh, I don't want to put you to sleep with my old memories."

"No, I love it when you tell me about yourself!"

"Then make sure you're sitting comfortably, because it's likely to be a long story. You'll get stiff and sore if you sit on the edge of the sofa like that. And you can put your cup down on the table, it will rest your fingers. Do you want me to tell you a secret? It takes time to learn to like tea. I didn't like the taste of it either when I first tried it."

"But how did you know?"

"Victoria, don't forget that I know everything!" said the former teacher, laughing.

Victoria smiled. Madame Françoise had said the same thing when they had first met in the attic.

"Well, then...where should I start? Have I ever talked to you about my sister, Laura?"

"No. I didn't know you had a sister."

"Well, I had a sister five years older than me. She lived here, with me, in this big house that we inherited from our parents. Laura died of cancer three years ago. Since then, I've been alone in the world, since neither of us ever married."

"And you don't have any children?"

"No," answered Madame Françoise, her eyes suddenly filled with sadness. "In my day, women who had children out of wedlock had a very bad reputation."

The old woman remained silent for a moment, lost in her memories. Then Victoria asked, "What did your sister do for a living?"

"Laura was also a teacher and since we both had all summer off we took advantage of it and travelled all over the world. We visited approximately twenty countries, a different one each year. As a tradition, on the last day of our trip, I would always buy a teacup to remind me of the country we had visited."

"What about the cup I chose? Where does it come from?"

"From a boutique in Paris, on the Rue de Rivoli, near the elegant tearoom called Chez Angelina. If you ever go there one day, you absolutely must taste their fabulous meringues. Just thinking about them makes my mouth water! And if you haven't acquired the taste for tea, you can always have a delicious hot chocolate."

Victoria thought that she would probably never be able to visit Paris. But in the meantime, she could dream about it thanks to Madame Françoise's stories.

"Did you know that in many countries, such as South America, sharing tea is a sign of friendship?"

"No, I didn't."

"Speaking of friendship, that reminds me... wait here, I'll be back in a moment."

Victoria watched the old woman walk slowly towards the two big glass doors that separated the sitting room from the dining room. Madame Françoise slid one of them back, it disappeared into the wall. Victoria had never seen such a thing before. And she still found it hard to believe that she was there, sitting on an antique sofa, drinking tea. Well, drinking wasn't exactly the right word, holding a cup of tea was more like it.

"Here!"

Victoria jumped. Lost in thought, she hadn't heard Madame Françoise return. Before Victoria had time to do a thing, the woman had taken her cup away and placed a box in her lap. It was carefully wrapped in shiny paper. The card said:

To my new friend Victoria,
Affectionately,
Madame Françoise

"What? Why?" exclaimed Victoria, surprised.

"Because it'll soon be Christmas. But mostly because you're important to me. Since you came into my life, you've brought back the sun. I have been alone since Laura died. You know, the weeks can be long when you have nobody to talk with, nobody to smile at. Now that I know you come to the attic on Monday evenings and we'll have a chance to chat for a few minutes, I spend my days waiting for that time. Well! Here I am again, going off on one of my tangents. Go on! Enough talking! Open your present," encouraged Madame Françoise, quickly wiping the corner of her eye with her lace handkerchief.

Victoria untied the ribbons and then gently loosened the paper so she wouldn't damage it.

"That's no way to unwrap a present! Tear that paper off!"

"Anyone would think you were the child here!" laughed Victoria.

"Indeed!" responded Madame Françoise in a dignified manner, her lips pursed.

Then she burst into joyful laughter while Victoria tore the wrapping paper to shreds. Then the young girl froze and tears came to her eyes.

"Don't you like the pastels and water-colours?"

"Yes, it's just that... I'm... so happy! Oh thank you, thank you!" exclaimed Victoria, throwing her arms around her new friend.

Madame Françoise hugged the girl tightly and sighed happily. It had been a long time since she'd been so happy.

"And I have a surprise for you too. I almost forgot!"

Victoria went out quickly to get the present she'd left on the hall table.

"This is to thank you for letting me use the attic. Merry Christmas! But be careful when you unwrap it, it's fragile."

"Alright. But you shouldn't have. I've already told you, I like the fact that you've set up your studio in that room."

Madame Françoise carefully untied the ribbon, undid the paper and unrolled its contents. What she saw left her dumbstruck, a rare event!

Madame Françoise admired the portrait of herself for a long time. In the black ink drawing, she was sitting in the attic rocking chair with her shawl around her shoulders and her hair pinned up in a tight bun, as it often was. What surprised her the most was that Victoria had drawn her with gentle eyes and a tender smile.

"It's beautiful, my dear. You have real talent. But how did you do it?" asked the old woman, with a lump in her throat.

"It was easy. After our very first meeting, I started with a sketch. The next Monday, I corrected some of the details, and so on and so on as the weeks went by. Then I used the pens and India ink that Julie gave me, and there you have it!"

"Would you like it if I had this drawing framed and hung it on the wall, right over the fireplace?"

"Really? Could I show the framed drawing to Julie before you put it up? I promised I'd show her what I did with the drawing materials she gave me."

"Of course. After Christmas."

"Speaking of Christmas, I might not be able to come back until January. You know, with Christmas dinner to prepare and the twins' birthday party... Mom will need my help."

"I understand perfectly. Your mother is lucky to have you."

"Well, I've got to go now."

Victoria headed towards the door and, when she was halfway there, turned back to Madame Françoise.

"Umm, would you give me another hug?"
"Of course, my dear! Come here."

Then, kissing Victoria gently on the forehead, Madame Françoise said, "Be careful going home."
"I will. Merry Christmas again!"

CHAPTER 8

The Invitation

"Mom?"

"Yes?"

"Can we invite Madame Françoise to our Christmas Eve dinner?"

"What? Invite that fussy old woman here? Have you lost your mind, Victoria?"

"But Mom, I told you, she's really nice and she'll be all alone for Christmas. She doesn't have any family."

"Victoria, you haven't really thought this through! Her here? In our tiny apartment? She's used to so much opulence... and the twins, they'd be really intimidated... and then there's Elizabeth, who's always up to something... no, I don't think it's a good idea."

"But..."

"Victoria, I said no!"

"You think she's a snob. But you're the one who is acting like a snob!"

Isabelle put her rolling pin down on the kitchen counter and wiped her floury hands on her apron. She walked over to her eldest daughter, put her hands on her shoulders, looked her in the eye and said,

"You can invite her if that'll make you happy, but I'm sure she'll refuse."

"We'll see! If you had the choice between spending Christmas Eve all alone in a big beautiful home or in a small apartment filled with warmth, joy and kids, which would you choose?"

Isabelle picked up her rolling pin again.

"Stop gabbing and let me cook. I've got a *tourtière* to make since it seems that we're going to have a visitor tomorrow."

"You're the best mother in the whole wide world!" cried Victoria, flinging her arms around her mother's neck.

"Hurry up and call Madame Ouellet to invite her, but first wipe the flour off your sweater or you'll track it all over the house."

"Yes, Mom. I love you!"

Ring, ring...

"Hello?"

"Hi, Madame Françoise!" said Victoria, excitedly.

"Oh, it's you! I didn't expect to hear from you for several days! What can I do for you?"

"I'm calling to invite you to celebrate Christmas Eve with us."

"What?"

"Yes, my mom, my brothers, my sister and I would like to invite you to come over at seven o'clock tomorrow evening to celebrate Christmas," repeated Victoria, patiently.

"I can't come!"

"Oh, why not? Are you going somewhere else?" Victoria asked, disappointed.

"No. I planned to go to midnight mass and then come back here and go to bed."

"So, what's stopping you from coming then?" Victoria asked boldly. "You could come to our house and then go to midnight mass. By then, the party will surely be over and the kids will be in bed."

"But I don't want to disturb your family celebration."

"But you wouldn't be disturbing it! Ple-e-e-ase!" pleaded Victoria.

"Is it okay with your mother?"

"Of course!"

"Then... I accept with pleasure," announced Madame Françoise, after hesitating one last moment.

"See you tomorrow then!"

"See you tomorrow, my dear."

The old woman put the receiver down gently. Her life had changed so much since she'd met Victoria! She felt as if she had a granddaughter, even though she never had any children of her own. Now... what could she get them? It was Christmas after all! Yesterday's gift didn't count, it was to show Victoria how much she enjoyed spending time with her. She suddenly had a great idea! Of course, that was it!

Victoria hung up the phone smiling. Her life had changed so much since she'd met Madame Françoise! She felt as if she finally had a grandmother, even though she'd never known her own grandparents. Now... what should she get for Madame Françoise? It was Christmas after all! Yesterday's drawing didn't count, it had been a thank you for letting her use the attic. She suddenly had a great idea! Of course, that was it!

CHAPTER 9

The Christmas Party

"Victoria, will you stop spinning around! You're making me dizzy."

"It's 6:55 and Madame Françoise should be here soon. You don't think she changed her mind, do you?"

"Well, look who's coming. Charles, when she knocks on the door, go and open it, please. And Edward, ask her for her coat and then go and put it on my bed. Okay, boys?"

"Mom, you look more nervous than I am."

"Maybe I am. I feel as if I am 11 years old again. I can't believe Fussy Françoise is going to celebrate Christmas at my place."

"Shh, Mom!"

"Hello," said the twins, as they opened the door.

"Hello, boys."

"Who are those presents for?" asked Elizabeth.

"They're for all of you," answered Madame Françoise.

"You're nice, Madame Fuss."

"Elizabeth!" cried Victoria and her mother in unison.

The old schoolteacher laughed. It had been a long time since she'd heard that nickname.

"Something smells wonderful! Thank you for inviting me. Isabelle, you haven't changed, you're still as beautiful as ever. Here, this is for you," continued Madame Françoise, handing Isabelle an enormous box filled with delicious chocolates.

"Thank you so much. Come, let's go into the living room. Boys, please take Madame Françoise's presents and put them under the tree."

"Yes, Mom."

The old woman hardly had time to sit down before Elizabeth came and stood in front of her, her thumb in her mouth. The little girl looked at her for a moment with her head tilted to one side and then suddenly said, "I have nice ovewaws, don't I?"

"Nice what?"

"She means overalls," corrected Victoria, embarrassed. "Elizabeth often mispronounces her words."

"They're really pretty," answered Madame Françoise.

Then, without asking if it was okay, the little girl climbed into the old woman's lap and asked her, "Where's Lizzie's present?"

"Elizabeth! We don't do that, it's very rude. Come here."

"No! I wanna stay with Madame Fanfuss."

"Ha! Ha! Ha! It's okay, she's so cute. You know, I had a lot of fun choosing your presents. I can hardly wait to give them to you. Can we do it now, Isabelle?"

"Yes! Yes!" exclaimed the children in unison.

"So, who should we begin with? The youngest? Elizabeth? Edward, could you please give me the red package that's right next to you?"

"Uh... I'm Charles. Here," he said, handing her the gift.

"I'm sorry. I promise I won't mix you up anymore! You both look so alike! Thank you, my dear. Here you go, Elizabeth."

The little girl opened her present quickly. It was a teddy bear almost as big as she was! Now it was the boys' turn. Charles, who was usually shy, dashed towards the tree, grinning from ear to ear. He picked up his gift and unwrapped a book called *The Little Prince* by Antoine de Saint-Exupéry. Then Edward followed his brother's example and found a magnificent book on dinosaurs.

"How did you know that Edward loves dinosaurs?" asked Victoria.

"I know because I listen to you when you talk to me. You told me that in the attic."

"Really? I don't remember."

"Well, even though I'm the old one, it seems you're the one who's losing her memory! Charles, can you bring me Victoria's present now please?"

"Another one? But you already gave me one!" exclaimed the girl.

"I know, but the day before yesterday was the day before yesterday. That doesn't count, tonight is Christmas Eve."

It was lucky that, the day before, Victoria had gone to the second-hand store.

"Wow! Thanks! These books are amazing. Now I'll be able to use my pastels and watercolours correctly."

"Promise me that your first work in colour will be for me. I still have lots of empty space on my walls!"

"I promise. And we also have a little present for you."

"You shouldn't have. Celebrating Christmas with you is already the most beautiful present I could receive."

"Here," said Victoria nervously, hoping Madame Françoise wouldn't notice the Made in Japan painted on the bottom.

"What a lovely teacup! Now, whenever I look at it or drink from it, I'll think of you and this wonderful Christmas Eve party. Thank you all!"

In the peaceful apartment, Isabelle cleaned up quietly. After keeping the whole family spellbound with her incredible stories, Madame Françoise had left with Victoria to attend midnight mass. They all had a wonderful time. The little ones were in bed. Isabelle couldn't believe it, even the twins felt comfortable with Madame Françoise. She'd changed so much since the time she was a teacher. Had the old woman mellowed with time or was it Isabelle who had matured? In any case, she'd really enjoyed spending time with the woman she'd rediscovered that evening. And what could she say about Elizabeth, who stuck to the old woman like glue?

Isabelle looked at the recipe book her guest had given her. It really was beautiful. She picked it up and flipped gently through the pages. A pink envelope fell out of the book. Her first name was written on it. Intrigued, she opened it.

Dear Isabelle,

Thank you for inviting me to celebrate Christmas with your lovely family. You can't imagine how happy the invitation has made me. Please accept this gift certificate and use it to organize a big birthday party for Charles and Edward.

Affectionately,
Fussy Françoise XXX

CHAPTER 10

The Accident

Monday at last! The twins' birthday party had gone very well. Victoria never imagined that they had so many friends! Her mother had outdone herself by preparing a delicious maple syrup cake. She'd found the recipe in the book Madame Françoise had given her for Christmas. Victoria could hardly wait to get to her studio and tell Madame Françoise all about the birthday party. She was impatient to be in her refuge once again and to continue her drawing as well. She'd set it aside for several weeks while she worked on Madame Françoise's portrait. But this evening, she was ready to get back to work on the drawing. The people were becoming clearer and clearer in her mind.

She glanced at the house. There were no lights on. The old woman must be waiting for her in the attic, sitting comfortably in the rocking chair.

"Hi Madame Françoise, it's me!"

There was no response. Victoria entered a dark, cold and empty room. A bad feeling came over her. Her heart was pounding a mile a minute. She ran over to the house.

"Ma-a-adame Fra-a-ançoise?"

Victoria knocked on the front door and turned the handle. The door wasn't locked. That wasn't normal. Something was really wrong. From the hallway, she could hear a feeble moan. Without taking off her boots, she raced towards the kitchen and then stopped dead in her tracks. She was paralyzed by the scene in front of her. Madame Françoise was lying on the floor. One of her legs was bent at an unnatural angle.

"There you are at last! Quickly, child, help me! Get the telephone, dial 911 and ask for help. My leg hurts, it hurts a lot," she said feebly.

Everything happened very quickly. The emergency technicians arrived quickly and carried Madame Françoise out to the ambulance. Victoria went with them. During the ride, she borrowed a mobile phone from one of the technicians and called her mother.

"Mom, I'm on my way to the hospital."
"Wh-What?!"
"Madame Françoise fell down when she was trying to get something off of the top shelf of the kitchen cupboard. I think her left leg is broken."
"Is she in a lot of pain?"
"Yes. She's conscious, but she isn't talking."
"If she's not talking, my God, it must be serious! I'll come and join you at the hospital right away. I'll ask Madame Beausoleil to look after the kids. What about you, sweetheart, are you okay?"

"Yes, Mom. But come quickly."

"I'm coming, little one. It's a good thing today's Monday!"

Isabelle arrived at the hospital emergency room a few minutes later and found Victoria huddled on a chair in the waiting room. When she saw her mother, the girl rushed into her arms. Only then did Victoria allow herself to cry.

"They've taken her to the operating room. She's not going to die, is she, Mom?" she hiccupped.

"No, honey. Let's stay positive while we wait for news from the doctor. I'm going to call Madame Beausoleil and tell her we'll be here for a while."

***

"Isabelle! Isabelle Mercier? Is that you?"

Victoria woke up with a start. She had dozed off, snuggled up next to her mother.

"Marc Daigle? What are you doing here? Are you a doctor?"

"Yes, I'm an orthopedic surgeon. I've just come out of the operating room. I came to give an update on my patient's condition to her family, and the nurse said it was you. Are you related to Françoise Ouellet?"

"No, we're friends."

"I could hardly believe my ears when I heard the name of the woman I was operating on. Fussy Françoise!"

Victoria didn't understand what was going on. The doctor seemed to know her mother and Madame Françoise.

"Marc, this is my daughter Victoria. Vicky, this is Dr. Daigle. We went to school together and we were both in Madame Françoise's class."

"And she was a terror," added the surgeon. "In those days, we used to believe that she could turn her head 270 degrees, like an owl. She always said she had eyes in the back of her head."

"Oh, Marc, if you only knew how much she's changed. Tell me, how is she?"

"Her leg is broken in two places. The operation went very well but, at her age, it will take a long time to heal. I hope she really has changed, because it will be a very long convalescence and the people who end up looking after her will need to be patient!"

CHAPTER 11

Emotional Storms

Victoria and Isabelle went to the hospital regularly to visit Madame Françoise. As Dr. Daigle had predicted, it was taking her a long time to recover from her accident.

"Hi there!" Victoria said cheerfully as she entered the patient's room.

"Hello, my dear. What are you doing here on a Monday? You should be up in the attic drawing. You know that I'm eager to see the famous picture."

"I'm going to start adding the colours soon. I must admit, I'm pretty proud of it."

"That's the important thing."

"Don't worry, you'll be the first to see it. I promise! But I'm here because I have a surprise for you."

"A surprise?"

"Yes. I was over at your house, watering the plants, when the phone rang. I thought it would be okay if I answered it."

"And?"

"It was the framing shop calling to say that your order was ready. I couldn't resist so I went and picked it up."

"That was very nice of you. I have no idea when I would've been able to get there myself. Did you bring the picture with you?"

"Yes. Wait here a minute. I'll go and get it, I left it in the hallway."

"And where do you think I might go, with my leg in a cast hanging in the air?" laughed Madame Françoise.

Then she added, more seriously, "According to the doctor, I won't be able to walk for several weeks. I really wonder how I'll..."

"Drum roll... dah-dah-dah-dah-dah-dah-dah!" interrupted Victoria. "Are you ready for the great unveiling?"

"Yes, my sweet," said Madame Françoise, forgetting her worries.

To keep Madame Françoise in suspense, Victoria removed the paper that covered the picture very slowly.

"Ta-dah! Madame... may I present the very first work of art by the young artist, Victoria Mercier-Laporte!"

The old woman laughed.

"You're so funny, Miss Show-off! Come closer so I can see your work of art."

After an emotional moment of silence, she said softly, "It's magnificent. Really, my dear, you've got talent. You should take art classes."

"Oh, you know, I like things fine the way they are. I draw for fun," answered Victoria, who knew very well that her mother couldn't afford to pay for drawing classes.

"I'll talk about it with your mom when she comes tomorrow."

"N-No. There's no need to bother her about that."

Victoria changed the subject:

"Can I show this picture to Julie, the graphic designer? I promised her I would."

"Of course!"

"Hello, Madame Ouellet. Hello, Victoria," said a male voice.

"Hello, Marc. I was expecting you earlier."

"Well, I was detained in the operating room by a nice gentleman. He also likes to perform acrobatic tricks. Except in his case, it's his right leg that's broken. I should introduce you to him, you'd make a good pair!"

"Don't even think about it, young man!" retorted Madame Françoise with a smile. "I'm too old for such things. What about you Marc, do you have a woman in your life?"

"No, I don't have the time."

"I can picture you with lovely Isabelle."

"Are you playing matchmaker now? I have a feeling your health is improving. Is Isabelle coming to see you soon?"

"Yes, tomorrow evening. Do you want to ask her out on a date?" she teased.

"No, my goodness! I want to talk to her about you."

Suddenly, Madame Françoise's high spirits vanished.

"Oh no, children, you're not going to go and start keeping things from me. Don't forget that I..."

"Know everything!" chorused Victoria and Dr. Daigle.

"Don't worry, we'll all discuss your return home together," concluded the doctor.

The next day, Dr. Daigle intercepted Isabelle just as she was about to enter Madame Françoise's room.

"Isabelle?"
"Hi, Marc! How are you?"
"Very well."

"Victoria said you wanted to talk to me about Madame Françoise's health."

"Yes... um... I know you're not legally responsible for her and you're not a member of her family, but you seem to care about her a lot."

"Yes, while visiting her, I've gotten to know her better and I really enjoy spending time with her. Furthermore, Victoria thinks of her as a grandmother."

"I need your advice. This evening, I have to tell her that she won't be able to live alone in that big house while she's recovering. We'll have to find her a place in a seniors residence while she rehabilitates. Normally, it's someone else's job to tell the patient, but in the case of Madame Ouellet, I feel I should do it. Will you come with me?"

"Oh God, how are we going to break the news to her? Are you sure there's no other option?"

"Unfortunately there isn't. It'll be a long time before she can walk again. In the meantime, she'll need help with everything."

Isabelle and Marc spent the next hour explaining the situation to Madame Françoise. She started out by getting angry, then she burst into tears. They tried to console her, and then a nurse came to look after her.

"Ugh, that wasn't easy," said Isabelle sadly, once the interview was over.

"No. You look exhausted. I've finished my shift for today... would you like to have a coffee at the little restaurant across the street?"

"Yes, that would do me good. Afterwards, I have to go home and explain everything to Victoria. She's looking after the children. She wanted to come along, but I said her place was at home this evening. She wasn't very happy about that."

"She's a very intelligent and mature girl for her age. I saw the portrait she did of Madame Ouellet. She's got talent. You should sign her up for art classes."

"Well, you know Marc, wanting to do something and being able to do something are two very different things."

CHAPTER 12

Coming Home

"Madame Françoise! Wanting to do something and being able to do something are two very different things. That's the craziest idea I've ever heard!" exclaimed Isabelle.

"Why?"

"It's not that I don't want to. It's that I can't. I have to work to feed and house my children."

"Oh, Mom, say yes!"

"Victoria, you keep out of this, please!"

"Isabelle... you don't understand. That's exactly what I'm offering you. A job, a full pantry and a house where your family can live."

"What? You don't really mean it?"

During the night, Madame Françoise had a brilliant idea. Why couldn't Isabelle, Victoria, the twins and Elizabeth come and live with her? There was plenty of room for everyone. Victoria would live right next door to her attic. The old woman would hire Isabelle to look after her full-time during her convalescence. That way, she wouldn't have to live in a seniors residence.

The two women asked Marc his opinion. After long discussions, Madame Françoise managed to convince them. The whole family would move into her big house for six months, until she could manage on her own again. During that time, the children would finish the school year. In July, when the tourist season started, Isabelle would easily be able to find a new job.

"I knew you'd agree!" said Madame Françoise triumphantly.

"That makes sense," admitted Isabelle, Marc and Victoria in unison. "You always know everything."

The week before Madame Françoise left the hospital, everyone worked very hard to rearrange her house. Bit by bit, Isabelle moved the children's toys and clothing. Everyone would have their own room, except the twins who didn't want to be separated. Everyone was excited.

Finally, the big day arrived. It was a real celebration. Balloons decorated the front doors. The house was lit up by Chinese lanterns. Madame Françoise was welcomed home as if she were a queen. As soon as Elizabeth saw her, she rushed to the wheelchair and tried to climb onto the old woman's lap.

"Elizabeth, no! You have to be careful of Madame Françoise's leg. I told you it wouldn't be easy with this little devil."

"Let her be. She's as light as a feather. Boys, push my wheelchair. We're going to take a tour of the house. I've missed it so much."

"Wow, do you ever have a lot of tea-cups!" said Edward, who hadn't been allowed to set foot in the sitting room before.

"Yes, my dear. Each cup is unique. If you would like, every evening after your bath, we'll come into the sitting room and you can choose one. Then I'll tell you its story. Would you like that?"

"Yea-a-ah!"

Madame Françoise kept her promise. Every evening, after the children had their baths, Isabelle lit a blazing fire in the fireplace. In their pyjamas, the kids sat on the comfortable rug and listened, fascinated, as the old woman talked about her adventures. Sometimes, when he could get away from work, Marc would join them. When that happened, Marc would carry Elizabeth up to bed, because she always fell asleep before the end of the story.

CHAPTER 13

A Real Family

Winter had given way to spring and soon it would be summer. The more time passed, the sadder Victoria became. She and her family would soon have to return to their little apartment. Just a few more weeks and it would all be over. They had gotten so used to having Madame Françoise there, in their lives, every day. She wasn't always patient, especially when her leg hurt, but that never lasted very long.

As for Isabelle, she had become more beautiful with each passing day. She wasn't as tired because she wasn't working nights anymore. Victoria thought that Marc the doctor also had something to do with it. She'd seen the glances they exchanged. And now that Madame Françoise was more independent, Isabelle spent a few hours of her time serving meals at the Breakfast Club. This gave her the opportunity to meet lots of interesting people.

The twins had changed too. They hadn't been sick all winter. Even Elizabeth was calmer. She no longer tried to attract everyone's attention. Anyway, Madame Françoise gave her plenty of that.

Victoria tried to concentrate once again on her drawing. She spent her time adding little details here and there. Her technique had improved a lot, especially since her mother had signed her up for lunch-hour drawing classes at school.

The young artist stood up, took a few steps back and studied her work with a critical eye. That was it. She was done at last.

Still, that didn't make her happy.

She sighed and decided to put her materials away and go home. As soon as she opened the front door, she sensed that something was going on. The atmosphere was strange.

"What's happening? Why have you been crying?" asked Victoria anxiously, when she saw her mother and Madame Françoise sitting at the table, each of them holding a wet Kleenex.

"Come and sit with us. Madame Françoise and I have to tell you something very important."

"Oh, no! I knew it. You want to tell me when we're leaving? Is that it?"

"That's it..." said her mother.

Victoria felt her eyes fill up with tears.

"Let's not leave the child in suspense, Isabelle."

"Okay, it's your idea, after all. You tell her."

"My darling, you won't be leaving."

"What?"

"First of all, we've all adapted so well to this new arrangement. I've never been so happy and, according to your mother, neither have all of you. The house, and my life, would be too empty without the sound of the boys bickering, without Elizabeth shouting and without you two. I always thought I would die alone and miserable in this big house. But since you've been living here, I've been feeling younger. If it hadn't been for that darned accident..."

"We wouldn't be here!"

"You're right, my dear."

Isabelle added, "The reason we were crying when you got here was because we were happy. Madame Françoise is offering me the possibility of starting my architecture classes again next fall. Since that's a few months away, there's still time for her health to improve. While I'm at university, Elizabeth will be at daycare."

"Who would have ever predicted that I'd have a family one day?" said Madame Françoise.

"What? You mean you didn't know? I thought you knew everything!"

"Marc! What are you doing here, you rascal? How long have you been here?"

"Long enough to hear the good news."

"Now we need to celebrate," decided Madame Françoise. "Go into the sitting room and choose your teacups while I make some tea!"

"Wait a minute. I'll be back," said Victoria.

She rushed out, filled with joy, and ran up to the attic. Five minutes later, when she entered the sitting room, everyone was there, even Elizabeth.

"Ahem. I've got something for you. I just finished it and I was waiting for a special moment to show it to you."

With her heart pounding, Victoria nervously turned the picture around. Finally, everyone was able to see the famous drawing they'd all heard so much about. On the right of the canvas was the old willow. Leaning against its gnarled old trunk, with her shoulders wrapped in her woollen shawl, was Madame Françoise smiling tenderly. At her feet, sitting on the grass among the wildflowers, were Victoria, Charles, Edward and Elizabeth, who seemed to hang on her words. A bit farther away, off to the left, Marc was offering a huge bouquet of daisies to Isabelle. Just above them all, in the deep blue sky, floated a big puffy cloud. And if you looked at it carefully, you could see the kind face of the children's father.

With her voice trembling with emotion, Madame Françoise said, "Victoria, you have drawn my dearest wish, which has now come true. A real family."

Sylvie Marcoux

Sylvie Marcoux worked for several years in the printing industry, first as a computer graphic designer and then as a production manager. In 2002, she published her first novel that won the Abitibi-Consolidated literary prize for children's books. In June 2004, Sylvie left the printing industry to join the team at the Saguenay-Lac-Saint-Jean book fair, where she acted as entertainment coordinator.

Since the release of her first book, she has made regular visits to schools and taken part in book fairs. This allows her to meet a lot of interesting people and, who knows, maybe even find inspiration for more stories. Sylvie loves telling stories so much!

Guadalupe Trejo

Guadalupe, a multidisciplinary artist, has always been fascinated by children's imaginations. She is a Montrealer with Mexican roots and has worked for several years in the visual communication field in both Montreal and Mexico City. Guadalupe also teaches photography to teenagers.

She is proud to be a member of the Éditions du Phoenix team and enjoys staying in touch with young people. Her illustrations are always inspired and original.

Mixed Sources
Product group from well-managed
forests and other controlled sources
www.fsc.org Cert no. SGS-COC-2624
© 1996 Forest Stewardship Council

Printed in September 2009
at Gauvin Press,
Gatineau, Québec